Words to Know Before You Read

begged

embarrassed

shopping

things

thought

wanted

wherever

www.rourkepublishing.com

Edited by Luana K. Mitten
Illustrated by Bob Reese
Art Direction and Page Layout by Renee Brady

Library of Congress Cataloging-in-Publication Data

Karapetkova, Holly
 But I want It / Holly Karapetkova.
     p. cm. -- (Little Birdie Books)
 ISBN 978-1-61741-818-1 (hard cover) (alk. paper)
 ISBN 978-1-61236-022-5 (soft cover)
 Library of Congress Control Number: 2011924695

Rourke Publishing
Printed in the United States of America, North Mankato, Minnesota
060711
060711CL

www.rourkepublishing.com - rourke@rourkepublishing.com
Post Office Box 643328 Vero Beach, Florida 32964

But I Want It!

By Holly Karapetkova

Illustrated by Bob Reese

Little Worm wanted a lot of things. Wherever he went, he wanted EVERYTHING!

When Little Worm saw Bird's giant acorn he screamed, "I WANT a giant acorn, too!"

"What would you do with a giant acorn? You don't need it," said Mother Worm.

9

When Little Worm's father took him to the park, he begged for an ice cream cone.

"No," said Father Worm. "You don't need ice cream before dinner."

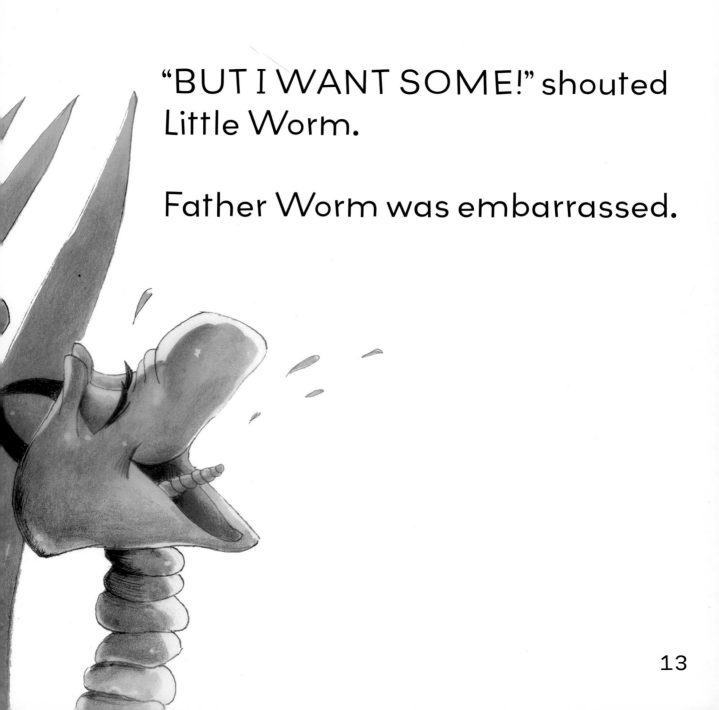

"BUT I WANT SOME!" shouted
Little Worm.

Father Worm was embarrassed.

That night, Mother and Father Worm talked to Little Worm, "Needs are things you must have to stay alive and healthy," said Father.

15

"Yes," said Father. "You don't need junk food and toys. Those are things you want."

"We get you what you need," said Mother. "But you have to stop begging for things you don't need."

A few days later, Little Worm went shopping with his mother.

"Look, Mom!" he said. "It's the new Super Worm movie!"

Then Little Worm stopped and thought for a moment. "I don't need that," he said.

Mother Worm smiled.

After Reading Activities

You and the Story...

How do you think Mother and Father Worm felt when Little Worm begged for things?

What lesson did Little Worm learn in this story?

Can you think of something that you wanted but didn't need?

Words You Know Now...

On a piece of paper write sentences with each of the words you know now.

begged	thought
embarrassed	wanted
shopping	wherever
things	

You Could... Make a List of Wants and Needs

- Divide a piece of paper in half.

- On one half write **wants**. On the other half write **needs**.

- On the **wants** half write a list of all the things you want.

- On the **needs** half write a list of all the things you **need**.

- Are there any things that can be on both lists?

About the Author

Holly Karapetkova lives in Virginia with her family and two dogs. She likes taking long walks in the park where she can think about wants and needs, and she loves writing books for kids.

About the Illustrator ?

Bob Reese began his art career at age 17 working for Walt Disney. His projects included the animated feature films Sleeping Beauty, The Sword and the Stone, and Paul Bunyan. He has also worked for Bob Clampett and Hanna Barbera Studios. He resides in Utah and enjoys spending time with his two daughters, five grandchildren, and cat named Venus.